FRIENDS
OF ACPL

Holt, Rinehart and Winston   *New York*

My Brother Fine With Me

LUCILLE CLIFTON

illustrated by
MONETA BARNETT

This is Baggy's book.   L.C.

To Lisa down the block.   M.B.

Library of Congress Cataloging in Publication Data
Clifton, Lucille,
    My brother fine with me.
    SUMMARY: When her five-year-old brother decides
to run away from home, Johnny is glad—at first.
    [1. Brothers and sisters—Fiction]   I. Barnett,
Moneta.   II. Title.
PZ7.C6224My   [E]   75-9621
ISBN 0-03-014171-0
date

About the Author
Lucille Clifton is an award-winning poet, and author of *Some of the Days of Everett Anderson, Everett Anderson's Christmas Coming, All Us Come Cross the Water, The Times They Used To Be,* and *Everett Anderson's Year.*

About the Artist
Moneta Barnett is a painter, illustrator, and designer. She has studied at Cooper Union and at the Brooklyn Museum Art School, and has worked as the art director of a serigraphic house, and in a design studio.

About the Book
The type was set in Baskerville with display in Souvenir Medium. The illustrations are pencil drawings.

My brother Baggy, he gonna run away. He say he tired of Mama and Daddy always telling him what to do. He say he a Black man, a warrior. And he can make it by hisself. So he gonna run away. I help him get his stuff together.

"You can come with me if you want to, Johnny," he say.
I'm named Johnetta after my Daddy. Baggy's real name
Wayne. I was the first-born child.

"That's O.K.," I say to Baggy. I don't want to run away 'cause I like it home O.K. The only problem I got at home is him and if he be gone it be fine with me. But I don't tell him that.

"Somebody have to stay here, see after the house while Mama and Daddy at work, Baggy. It might as well be me, long as I'm already the oldest and all."

"O.K.," Baggy say.

Me and Baggy the only children. I was the only child till
he come being born. Everything was all right, me and Mama
and Daddy doing fine till Mama come spreading out like a
pancake and Aunt Winnie who don't even like children
come to watch me for a while and Mama go off and come
back here with Baggy. I was mad for a long time and I ain't
really all that glad now, but I don't let on. I'm eight years
old and he five.

I help him get his stuff together for the running away. He don't even know what he need. He ain't got nothing but a whistle and his pick. I put in his toothbrush and a wash-cloth. He get all his minibike pictures. He collects them.

"When I get there I'm gonna have to get me a minibike, Johnny."

"Well, where you running off to anyhow, Baggy?"

He grin all simple.

"Don't you worry 'bout me none, girl."

Shoot, I ain't even worried about him, I be just as glad he gone. Me and him put all his stuff in a shopping bag, and he get his bat and he ready to go. He want to be gone before Mama and Daddy get home from work. He most probably get a whipping if they catch him with the good washcloth.

"Well, Baggy, this is it, I guess," I say.

"Yeah, well, Johnny, you try to keep on making it and I'll write you soon as I get there," he say.

"O.K.," I say. And he gone.

Mama and Daddy both work and my job in the summer is to take care of Baggy till they get home. During the winter me and him both go to school and before he was old enough for nursery Mama stayed home but soon as he old enough she went back to work. She say she just as glad. Summertime I got to watch him, though, and even when I get to go out and play I got to drag him with me. He a drag.

Now he done run away, and I feel just like Dr. King say, free at last.

I figure I'll clean up some and then Mama and Daddy won't feel so bad when they get home and he gone. I figure they'll miss him some at first but they get over it and then it be just like the old days. Just us. Mama and Daddy and me. It be fine.

Cleaning up me and Baggy's room a snap now he done took all them old minibike pictures off the floor and under the bed and everyplace. Me and him be looking at them all night and he be making motor sounds so somebody can't hardly get to sleep. Guess I'll get to sleep easy now but I don't know. I hope so. I can't sleep good if it's real quiet 'cause I be scared. Specially by myself. Shoot.

I figure I'll make me some lunch and then clean up the
kitchen and then go on out. I got a girlfriend name Peaches
and she be waiting for me everyday. She got to watch her
little sister and me and Peaches take the kids over to the
schoolyard and we can talk while they swing and carry on.
They have a good time too.

Shoot. I forgot. We can't go over there if ain't nobody for
Peaches' little sister to play with.

Shoot.

I love tuna fish. I'll make me a tuna fish sandwich for lunch. We always get tuna fish for me and peanut butter and jelly for Baggy. Shoot, now what we gonna do with all this peanut butter and jelly? Don't nobody around here like the stuff but old simple Baggy. We gonna have a house full of old stale peanut butter and jelly.

That Baggy always messing up. Before he come around here I never did have to think about his old sandwiches and who Peaches' little sister gonna play with and how am I gonna get to sleep. Before he come along it was just me by myself. By myself. Shoot.

I may as well go on out and wait for Mama and Daddy on the step. Ain't nothing else to do around here. Ain't no fun around here by yourself. Peaches just get on my nerves. She think she cute anyhow. Her and her simple little sister. Baggy can beat her up any day. If he want to.

Lord have mercy, my brother Baggy out here sitting on the step!

"What you doing out here, Baggy?" I say.

"I been thinking 'bout things, Johnny," he say. "When I get there I'm gonna be so much worried 'bout you all the time I won't be able to get me my minibike or nothing."

"I'm sorry, Baggy," I say.

"Seem to me, a warrior better stay home and take care of his family." I grin when he say that.

"O.K., Baggy," I say, "you may as well not run away."

"O.K.," he say, "O.K. I'm gonna go get me a peanut butter and jelly."

I'm real glad. I done got used to him, you know. My brother fine with me.